Phoebe G. Green

A Passport to Pastries!

Phoebe G. Green
A Passport to Pastries!

VEERA HiRANANDANi
illustrated by CHRISTINE ALMEDA

PENGUIN WORKSHOP

PENGUIN WORKSHOP
An Imprint of Penguin Random House LLC, New York

Text copyright © 2015 by Veera Hiranandani. Illustrations copyright © 2020 by Penguin Random House LLC. All rights reserved. First published in 2015 by Grosset & Dunlap. This edition published in 2020 by Penguin Workshop, an imprint of Penguin Random House LLC, New York. PENGUIN and PENGUIN WORKSHOP are trademarks of Penguin Books Ltd, and the W colophon is a registered trademark of Penguin Random House LLC. Printed in the USA.

Visit us online at www.penguinrandomhouse.com.

Library of Congress Control Number: 2014043478

ISBN 9780593096932 (paperback)   10 9 8 7 6 5 4 3 2 1
ISBN 9780593096949 (library binding)   10 9 8 7 6 5 4 3 2 1

For **David, Hannah, and Eli,**
my best readers and eaters
—VH

For **Aeden and his sweet tooth**
—CA

Chapter One

My name is Phoebe G. Green, and I have a new nickname! My dad made it up. Get ready for it: Phoebe Green, The List Queen. Pretty cool, huh? It's an extra-special nickname because it's actually longer than my regular name. Usually nicknames are shorter, like Pheebs. I'm always making lists, so that's why my dad calls me The List Queen. Mostly I

make lists about why I'm so lucky, but
this week I had to make an unlucky
list. It was just that kind of week.
Here's why:

1 I didn't do well on my
spelling test last week,
so my parents made
me do very boring
spelling flash
cards.
2 For some reason,
the more I do very boring
spelling flash cards, the more
I think about what to make
for lunch.

Once I thought about how artichokes and tomatoes and melty mozzarella cheese would taste in a toasty wrap. (By the way, I'm a foodie, which means I like eating and cooking delicious things . . . a lot.)

3 Then I got a bad cold and didn't go to school for two days. My nose was so stuffed that food tasted like paper, which was the saddest thing ever.

4 Because I was sick, I missed Charlotte Hempler's birthday party, so I didn't get to eat the homemade cupcakes her mom brought us. They might have tasted like paper because of my cold, but still. Then I finally felt better. So I made a wrap and brought it to school, but it opened up while I was eating it, and I got tomato juice all over my favorite purple T-shirt.

But then, everything changed at dinner one night. We ate yummy salmon (which is my favorite fish because it tastes very buttery even though there's no butter in it), baked potatoes, and sautéed spinach (that's a fancy way of saying spinach cooked in a pan). I helped Dad make all of it because we are the official family chefs now. One of my best friends, Camille, is the reason why I like food so much. She moved to my town all the way from France and brought these beautiful French lunches to school. I loved them, even though lots of people thought they were

weird. Then I became a foodie, Camille and I became best friends, and Dad and I became the family chefs. My mom never liked cooking that much, so it worked out.

During dinner, I started thinking about my boring spelling cards again.

"Mom, I don't understand why I have spelling tests," I said. "When I use the computer, it always fixes my wrong words."

"Phoebe," my mom said, "knowing how to spell is part of learning English."

"But, Mom, things are different in the digital age," I said because I heard someone saying "digital age" on TV yesterday, and I thought it sounded cool, even though I didn't really know what it meant. Mom, Dad, and my older sister, Molly, stopped chewing their salmon and blinked at me. I guess they didn't know what it meant, either. Then Mom told us something very interesting.

"I spoke to Isabelle Durand today," she said as she took a bite of spinach.

Isabelle Durand is Camille's mom. I also have another best friend, named Sage, who is not French at all, but he does like french fries a lot.

"Did Camille invite me for another playdate?" I started bouncing up and down.

"This is even better," Mom said. "February break is coming up, and you know how we normally visit Grandma Green in Miami?"

"Yeah, yeah?" I said, almost yelling. I loved going to Miami. The pool there was really warm, and everyone was so

old and nice and let me play cards with
them.

"This year, I think we might go
somewhere else," she said, grinning,
and now looking at Dad.

"Where?" Molly asked. "London?"
Molly's best friend, Maya, went to
London last year, and Molly hasn't
stopped talking about it.

"Close. The Durands invited us to France for Camille's birthday!" Mom said excitedly. "Camille's grandmother has a house right outside Paris where we could all stay."

"It's a wonderful opportunity," Dad said, smiling extra big.

"Paris?" Molly said, and clapped her hands together. "That's even better than London!"

"Wow," I said, letting it sink in. "Does Camille's grandmother live in a really fancy French place like a castle?" I asked.

"I'm sure it's very nice, Phoebe, but I don't think it's a castle," Dad said.

"I can't wait to tell Maya!" Molly exclaimed.

Dad started to clean up the plates. "So what do you think, Phoebe?"

At first I felt sad about not going to Miami, but then I thought about walking on French streets and eating all the foods I've had at Camille's house, like goat cheese, duck, and ratatouille (it's a delicious vegetable stew that Camille's dad made for us once that doesn't even have rats in it).

"I want to go!" I said, smiling.

So that's when my week started to get lucky again. Pretty cool, huh?

The next day, I was walking to school with Sage and wanted to tell him about going to France with Camille. But I wasn't sure if he'd be jealous. I also didn't want to talk to Camille about France until I told Sage. So I decided to stay away from both of them in the morning and look for things in my cubby until my teacher, Mrs. B, called morning  meeting. That's when everyone sits crisscross applesauce on the rug, and she tells us the plan for the day. We have to be very quiet, which I normally don't like, but today I didn't mind.

Lunch was trickier, since Sage, Camille, and I usually sit together. So I decided to fall off the monkey bars at recess and pretend to bump my knee. Then I could eat lunch in the nurse's office with an ice pack. The only problem was that when I pretended to fall off the monkey bars and hurt my knee, I actually hurt my knee. After

being at the nurse's office, I tried to walk back to my classroom without Camille and Sage seeing me, but just as I was going around the corner, our whole class came in from recess. I tried to rush ahead, but I was limping because my knee still hurt. Camille and Sage caught up with me.

"Phoebe, is something wrong?" Camille asked, blinking her long eyelashes.

"Yeah, all morning you've acted like you don't want to talk to us," Sage said, and looked me right in the eye, which makes me very nervous.

"Guys, nothing's wrong. I just—" Then I put my hand over my mouth.

"What?" they both said at the same

time. Sage nicely took my hand away from my mouth.

"Sage, I'm going to France with Camille's family in February. Camille, I didn't want to talk about it with you until I told Sage," I said loudly. Then I swallowed. "That's all."

"You are?" Sage said.

I nodded.

"Oh!" Camille said, clasping her hands together. "So that means you're definitely coming?"

"Yeah! My dad said it's a wonderful opportunity!" I stood up tall.

"Why didn't you want to tell me?" Sage asked.

I thought for a second. "Because I was afraid you'd be jealous. Aren't you?"

Sage looked up and thought for a moment. "I guess a little," he said.

"Not a lot?" I asked, starting to feel a bit mad.

"But I don't want anyone to be jealous," Camille interrupted in her worried way. "Maybe you could come, too, Sage."

I jumped up and down and clapped my hands. Going to a whole other country with Sage and Camille would be the best thing that's ever happened in the whole history of everything!

"Yeah!" Sage said, and started jumping, too. "Oh, but wait," he said.

We stopped jumping.

"We always visit my cousins and go skiing over the winter break." He looked down.

"Oh, too bad," Camille said with her head down.

"Now I am really jealous," Sage said.

I smiled.

"Maybe we could be jealous of

your ski trip, too," Camille suggested, looking more cheerful.

"That's a perfect idea!" I said. I didn't even know Camille could have perfect ideas like that. So we all agreed to be jealous and that way no one got left out. I'm lucky to have such great best friends.

Chapter Two

It was finally the day of our trip to Paris. My eyes popped open as soon as the sun came up. I immediately jumped out of bed and started trying on clothes. I wanted to look super French for the trip, so I thought about Camille's mom. She acted Frencher than Camille and always wore a lot of black clothes, but not in a scary witch way, just in a fancy French lady way. While I tried on French-looking clothes, I thought about the five very important things Camille taught me to say in French:

1. S'il vous plaît (Please)
2. Merci (Thank you)
3. Bonjour (Hello)
4. Au revoir (Good-bye)
5. Je m'appelle Phoebe. (My name is Phoebe.)

"Phoebe, we're leaving right now. We have to meet the Durands at the airport!" Mom called in her very high-pitched voice that she saves for trips.

I rushed downstairs in black dance

tights and a black
leotard because those
were all the black
clothes I could
find. I was
also wearing
a beret, which
is a black hat

that French people wear. I know that
because I have a book about France that
Mom bought me for the trip. Molly says
most French people don't really wear
berets. She takes French in school, so
she thinks she knows everything. But
in the book, lots of people wear berets,
so I know Molly's wrong.

"Phoebe!" Mom said, now pretty much screaming. "Our flight leaves in two hours, and you're not wearing any pants!"

I looked down. "I'm all covered, and I think I look very French," I said. "Don't I?"

Mom opened her mouth to say something and then closed it and threw her hands up in the air.

Molly was behind me and pulled me away from Mom. "Come on," she whispered in my ear. "I'll help you find something. If we don't get in the car quick, Mom's going to explode."

I nodded and followed her. She helped me find a red skirt that she said looked very chic with my outfit. I wasn't sure what "chic" meant, but it sounded nice. Sometimes Molly could be a pretty cool big sister even if she was a know-it-all.

We all finally got in the car and zoomed away. Then Mom yelled out, "Oh no!"

And Dad yelled out, "What?"

"Our passports!" Mom yelled back.

Passports are these neat little books with your picture inside them to remind you who you are. Mom says they don't let you leave the country without them.

So we zoomed back to the house,
and Mom ran inside and got the
passports. Then we zoomed away again,
this time for good.

Once we got to the airport and through
all the guards who X-ray you and look at
your passport and then back at you and
then back at your passport over and over,
Mom calmed down. Then we saw the
Durands at the airplane gate.

Camille came running over extra
excited, wearing her red dress and a dark
blue coat.

"You look very chic!" I said, feeling
extra excited, too. I still wasn't sure
what that meant, but I assumed it meant

something French and nice.

"Thanks!" she said. "I can't wait to show you my grandmother's house."

"I can't wait to see it!" I said, and then we jumped up and down and

 hugged because going to France with one of your best friends makes you want to jump up and down and hug a lot.

"Phoebe, my, my," said Mrs. Durand, who was wearing a black sweater, black pants, and a red coat. "Look at you!"

"See, Mom, I do look very French.
Mrs. Durand looks just like me!"

Mom and Mrs. Durand smiled at
each other.

"But I am missing my beret,"
Mrs. Durand said, and touched the top
of her head.

"That's okay," I said to Mrs. Durand.
"You can borrow mine if you want."

On the plane, Camille and I got to sit together in a three-people row with Molly, but Molly wanted to read her books and listen to her thirteen-year-old rock music, so she put her earphones on.

I turned to Camille and showed her my list of foods I wanted to try in France:

1 Baguettes (They're not little bags. They are long loaves of bread that look like baseball bats.)
2 Tarte tatin (It's an upside-down apple pie that someone must have made by mistake.)
3 Madeleine cookies (They sound so friendly, don't they?)

4 Quiche (I've had it before, but I want to try a real French quiche. It's kind of like an egg pie.)

5 Bouillabaisse (It's some kind of fish stew, but mostly it's just fun to say. Bool-ya-base!)

6 The Eiffel Tower (It's not a food, but it's always been my dream to walk up all the way to the top. At least it's been

my dream since last Thursday
when Mom told me you could.)

Camille looked at the list and nodded
excitedly. "I love all these foods, too.
We're so alike. That's why we're best
friends!"

I smiled. "What's your favorite
French food ever?" I asked.

"You'll see," Camille said, "at my
birthday dinner." Then she pointed to
the last thing on my list. "I've never
walked up the Eiffel Tower, either.
Maybe we could do it together?!"

"Okay," I said. But secretly I thought,
what kind of French person has never

walked up the Eiffel Tower?! I also thought about what Camille said about us being so alike. Is that really why we were best friends?

After a very long time of card playing and trying to nap on the small lumpy airplane pillows they gave out for free, eating snacks with fancy French words on the package, and watching movies, we finally landed. I kept the earphones and a bag of nuts with French writing on it so I'd always remember my first plane trip out of my whole country and into another one. I tried to keep the pillow, but the airplane people said I had to give it back. In the French airport, not one person was in a beret. Maybe we flew to the wrong country by mistake?!

The Durands rented a big car for all of us. As we drove through Paris, I could see the Eiffel Tower behind us, so I knew we were definitely in France.

"Hi, Eiffel Tower!" I called out, waving. I still didn't see anyone wearing a beret, though.

When we got out of the city, I started looking for a big, fancy house.

My mom said not to get my hopes up, but I couldn't keep my hopes down. They just kept going up.

We turned on to a little dirt road.

"Is there going to be a gate?" I asked. Camille looked at me.

"A gate?" she said.

"You know, in front of the house?" I asked because fancy houses always have gates. At least they do in storybooks.

"There's no gate," Camille said, looking confused.

We pulled up in front of a little stone house, which was cute but not that big or fancy and did not have a gate in front of it. No berets. No gate. No fancy house. Maybe France was going to be a little different than I thought.

Chapter Three

Camille's grandmother, who Camille called Mémé, came out of the house, waving. *"Bonjour, bonjour!"* she said. She wore white pants and a black sweater, and had her silvery hair in a bun. After she hugged everyone, she held my face with both of her hands. *"Comme elle est adorable!"* she said. I smiled and nodded even though I had no idea what she was saying. Camille told me later that it meant "She's so cute!"

"*S'il vous plaît, merci, bonjour, au revoir, je m'appelle* Phoebe," I blurted out.

Mémé smiled blankly. "Excuse me?" she said, turning to Camille.

I didn't realize that Camille's grandmother would speak English. "I just wanted to say all the French words I know in case I don't get to say them later," I said to both of them.

Camille laughed, "Come on, Phoebe, I'll

show you around," she said, and pulled me in the door. Inside the little stone house there was a living room, a kitchen, and two bedrooms on the first floor. Lace curtains covered all the windows. There was a small wooden table and four blue chairs in the middle of the bright yellow kitchen. The whole house smelled like butter, and I saw a yummy-looking pie thing cooling on the counter.

"This is the prettiest house I've ever seen, even if it's not that big and fancy!" I almost shouted.

Camille smiled. "Want to see where we're going to sleep?" she said. I nodded and followed her upstairs.

We walked into a room to the right of the stairs. There was another room across the hall where my parents were going to sleep. I looked around the teeny, tiny room. There were two small white beds, a dresser in between, and a mattress on the floor. On each bed there was a doll.

"Is this a room for the dolls or for us?" I asked.

"It's for us, silly," Camille said.

"These quilts are extra flowery," I said, smoothing my hand over the quilt on one bed. "And the ceilings are so low and slanty. It's kind of like being inside a dollhouse for real."

"I know. The quilts are antiques," Camille said in a serious voice, so I nodded in a serious way because it seemed like *antique* was a very serious word.

Camille suddenly dove for her dolls. She hugged them tightly.

"I thought you just liked fairies," I said. Camille had a fairy collection at home.

"Well, they're my favorite, but I love all kinds of dolls. Mémé keeps these for me for when I visit," she explained.

"This is Juliette and this is Josephine. You can hold Josephine when you sleep," she told me, putting a doll wearing a purple sparkly dress in my arms.

"Okay," I said, taking Josephine. Her dress was a little scratchy. I was more of a stuffed-animal person, but I didn't want Camille to think I didn't like dolls.

"This room is so cute!" Molly said when she came upstairs. "Your dolls are beautiful, Camille." Camille's face turned red.

"Thank you!" Camille said. "They were my mom's when she was little. They're really old and delicate."

"Oh wow! Can I see one? I promise I'll be careful," Molly said.

"You can have mine," I said, and gave her Josephine.

"You don't like her?" Camille asked, looking a little sad.

"No, I love her," I said quickly. "I just wanted Molly to see." Molly was the one who really liked dolls and still kept a bunch of Barbies and an American Girl doll stuffed in the back of her closet that she thought nobody knew about.

Molly sat next to Camille, and
Camille told her all about the dolls,
pointing out different parts of their
clothes. I felt like I could stand on my
head and they wouldn't even notice. I
made a couple of loud sighing sounds,
but they didn't look up, so I decided to
go downstairs.

The grown-ups were sitting in the living room around a table with little bowls of nuts, olives, and crackers.

I grabbed a salty olive and poked my head in the kitchen. I looked at the pie on the counter. It was sort of brown and caramel colored. I couldn't tell what it was, and it didn't seem too hot, so I stuck my pinky in the corner and licked it. Yum. It tasted like apples. Maybe it was a tarte tatin!

"You like cooking?" a French voice said over

my shoulder. I whipped around. It was Mémé.

"Oh yes," I said, my pinkie still in my mouth. "I was just . . ."

She smiled. "It's okay. Food is meant to be tasted. Your parents tell me you are, how do you say, a foodie?" Mémé said, putting on a yellow apron.

"I am! But don't worry, it just means I really like food," I said.

"Oh, I'm not worried. I know all about foodies," she said, smiling at me. "That is a tarte tatin." She pointed to the apple thingy I just stuck my finger in.

"I knew it!" I said.

"Hi, Mémé," Camille said behind

me. "I smell *poulet fricassée!*"

My heart did a happy flip when I saw Camille. I was worried she would want to spend the rest of the afternoon showing Molly her dolls.

"Oui, ma chérie," Mémé said, and gently patted Camille's cheek. She stirred some buttery, lemony-smelling chicken in a pan.

"Wait, does 'poulay' mean chicken?" I asked.

"Oui!" Mémé said.

"So is the rest of the stuff in there 'freecasay'?" I wondered, pointing to the pan.

Mémé chuckled. "That's the sauce I

made with vegetables, herbs, lemon juice, butter, broth, and just a touch of cream."

"Can Phoebe and I help you with the rest of dinner?" Camille asked.

"Please," Mémé said as she put the lid on the pan of chicken. In a minute she had us chopping up a shallot into teeny, tiny pieces for a salad dressing. I had never even seen a shallot before. It's kind of like an onion and kind of like garlic. Then we stirred in the olive oil, vinegar, mustard, salt, and pepper. We also chopped up some parsley and put that in. We mixed and mixed, and it looked greenish and oily and a little goopy. Then Mémé dipped in some lettuce for us each to taste.

"It's good enough to drink!" I exclaimed.

"Yes, but please don't drink it!" Mémé said, looking worried.

"Don't worry, Mémé," said Camille.

"I would never drink salad dressing,

unless I was *really* thirsty," I said, and
Camille and I giggled. Maybe I didn't
love dolls as much as Camille did, but
we both really liked food.

"What's in the oven?" I asked.

"It's a cheese soufflé," Mémé said.

"A *sooflay*," I said. "That's fun to say.
Sooflay, sooflay, sooflay."

"Soufflé, soufflé, soufflé!" Camille
said, and then this happened:

❶ We held hands and danced around the kitchen singing "soufflé, soufflé, soufflé!" and Mémé started laughing.

❷ We let go, and I danced over to the oven to look through the glass window.

❸ The soufflé looked so puffy I thought it might explode.

❹ I opened the oven quickly and

luckily the soufflé didn't look so puffy anymore.

5 Then Camille came over, and Mémé said, "non, non! My soufflé!"

I swallowed hard.

"You shouldn't open the oven. You could get burned," Mémé said to me, her hands on her hips.

"I'm sorry," I said, and looked down at my feet. I don't know why I did it. At home I'm not allowed to open the oven, either.

"Mémé, don't be mad at Phoebe. She just gets excited."

"It's true," I explained. "My parents tell me I get overstimulated, which means extra excited."

Mémé's face softened. She took in a deep breath and let it out. People are always taking deep breaths at me, especially grown-ups.

"It's okay, it will still taste good," she said, and patted my arm. "Why don't you both go play for a little while?" She waved her hand toward the living room.

Camille nodded. Then we went back upstairs and sat on our beds quietly.

"Don't worry about Mémé," she said after a minute. "She's just very serious about her food."

"So am I," I said. "I only wanted to help."

"You did. The salad dressing is good enough to drink!" Camille said, and bounced on her bed. I smiled. Camille was a little bouncier and louder in France, and I liked that. Maybe now that we were best friends, we were becoming more the same.

"Want to play with Juliette and Josephine?" she asked.

"Sure," I said.

We made up a story where Juliette and Josephine were best friends, did everything together, and liked all the same things. We did that until dinner and it wasn't even boring.

Dinner was super yummy. I told Mémé that the cheese soufflé was my favorite even if it wasn't puffy anymore. Everyone at the table laughed, especially Mémé.

"Tomorrow, we'll visit my old pastry shop and have a look around. You can try anything you want, Phoebe," said Mr. Durand after dinner.

"Really? Anything?" My eyes almost popped out of my head.

"Yes," he said, "but our specialty is chocolate croissants, so you must try those!"

That sounded delicious, but suddenly my eyes felt very heavy.

"I think you both have a serious case of jet lag," Mom said. "Let's get you to sleep."

"Jet lag?" I said sleepily.

"Don't worry. Happens to everybody when they change time zones," Mrs. Durand said.

I was too sleepy to ask any more questions. Our moms walked us up the stairs and helped us find our pj's. We brushed our teeth and fell into bed.

"France is the best," I whispered to Camille as we lay there.

"That's exactly what I was thinking," Camille said.

As we drifted off to sleep, I thought about the piles of chocolate croissants, tarts, and mounds of whipped cream I would taste tomorrow. I couldn't wait to tell Sage.

Chapter Four

The next morning, Mémé set out homemade baguettes with butter and strawberry jam.

"If breakfast in France is this good, I can't wait to see what the rest of the day is going to be like," I said, biting into a big slice of warm crunchy-on-the-outside bread covered in butter and jam. "This just might be the best day of my life," I continued with my mouth full, little crumbs of bread flying out of me. Mémé handed me a napkin. But the baguette wasn't even the best part. The best part was the hot chocolate. Mémé served it to us in bowls. At first I thought she was tired and made a mistake, but Camille said it's what French people do. Pretty cool, huh?

"It's like drinking milk from a cereal bowl, but even better," I said between slurps of creamy warm chocolate.

"Why?" Molly asked.

"Because nobody tells you to stop."

Mémé smiled and patted me on the head. Then she went over and patted Camille and Molly on the head, too. Mémé really liked patting people.

"So how about some sightseeing today?" Mrs. Durand said. "Maybe the Louvre, the pastry shop, then a little shopping?"

"Did I hear shopping?" Molly said, with practically her whole face in her bowl of hot chocolate.

"Along with some other things," Dad said.

"I want to go to the Eiffel Tower," I said.

"We'll try to see it later in the week," said Mom. "We have a lot of other things to see first."

"But I've been dreaming about it for so long," I said.

"You didn't even know about it until a week ago, Phoebe," Dad said.

"A week is a long time in kid years," I said, because I once heard my mom say that. Dad shook his head.

When we left for Paris,

Mémé stayed home because she'd already seen everything. We took a train to the Louvre, which is a museum that's as big as a soccer field. It also has a huge glass pyramid in front that you get to walk through, some funny naked statues, and a famous picture of a lady who doesn't really know how to smile. It was fun at  first but got boring after a while.

Afterward we went to Mr. Durand's old *patisserie*, which is a fancy French word for a pastry shop. Mom and Molly decided to look at a few stores we saw on the way and meet up with us a little later.

Mr. Durand's friend owned the patisserie now. When I walked in, a cloud of butter, sugar, caramel, chocolate, and nuts blended and hit me smack in the nose. Inside the glass cases were the most beautiful cakes, cookies, and tarts I'd ever seen. There was also a big tray of chocolate croissants on the counter under a glass cover.

"I want to eat everything!" I yelled. Everyone in the shop turned and looked at me. Dad smiled, and his cheeks even got a little red. I've never seen that happen to Dad.

Mr. Durand said hello to the lady behind the counter. "Before we try some things, how would you like to see the kitchen?" he asked me.

"I would, I would." I was jumping

up and down now. Then I grabbed Camille's hand and we jumped some more. We all followed Mr. Durand behind the counter into the kitchen.

"I've never been *behind* a counter," I whispered to Camille.

Camille giggled as we walked in back. "Isn't it wonderful?" she whispered, pointing toward the kitchen. "I used to practically live here."

I looked around. It smelled even more chocolaty and buttery than in the front. There were two people in white aprons working on the metal counters. A man rolled out dough and a woman was squeezing out chocolate

icing designs on a big pink-
frosted cake. On the side
of one counter there was
a big tray of colorful fruit
tarts, and a tray of white-
frosted cookies with silver dots on them.

"Monsieur Martin is the best croissant
maker in all of France," Mr. Durand said,
and shook the man's hand.

"He exaggerates," Monsieur Martin
said.

"I exaggerate, too!" I said. "At least my
dad is always telling me that."

"Phoebe, I think you might be
exaggerating," Dad said, his cheeks
getting red again.

Monsieur Martin smiled. "And who is this young exaggerator?" he asked.

"This is Camille's friend Phoebe," Mr. Durand said.

"Nice to meet you, Phoebe. Would you like to learn how to make a chocolate croissant?"

"Oh yes, almost as much as I want

to eat one," I said. Monsieur Martin laughed. Then he had me and Camille wash our hands and put on aprons like real chefs. He showed us how to flatten out the butter on top of the dough and fold the dough over the butter. The dough already seemed pretty buttery, but I guess French people like to put butter on their butter. Then we put the dough in the refrigerator, and he took out some other dough that already had the butter in it. We rolled that out, and he cut it into triangles with a little wheel on a stick, kind of like a pizza cutter. We each had a turn. This is what happened when I tried:

1 My triangles looked more like rectangles.

❷ The dough kept sticking to the roller no matter how much I told it not to.

❸ When I tried to roll them up, the dough mushed together into a big blob.

❹ Finally, I cut one into a good triangle and put the chocolate on. I rolled it up, and it didn't stick at all, but then I got so excited I knocked a little dish of melted butter over and made a big mess.

I looked over at Camille. She had already cut a bunch of triangles out of her dough and was sprinkling on the chocolate and rolling them up like it was no big deal.

"You're really good at that," I said.

"Thanks," she said back to me.

"I don't think I'll ever be as good as you," I said. We definitely weren't alike this way.

"You're good at lots of things,"
she said. But she didn't say what I was
good at.

"It's okay, Phoebe. It takes practice.
It only took me twenty years to learn,"
Mr. Durand said, grinning. Dad laughed
kind of extra loud. Camille gave me a
little smile. I tried to smile back, but
I felt an eensy-weensy bit jealous of
them and their super croissant-making
powers.

When the dough triangles were
baking, we tasted little pieces of some
other things, like cookies, fruit tarts, and
chocolate éclairs, which looked like little
chocolate hot dogs with custard inside.

They were all delicious, but I couldn't wait to try the chocolate croissants. The smell of them baking in the oven was making me dizzy in a happy way. I almost didn't care anymore about how bad I was at making them. Almost.

Finally, they were ready. As we tasted them, it got very quiet. They were so flaky and buttery. The warm melted chocolate in  the center surprised my tongue. It was so good, I almost fainted. I asked my dad if we could take one home to Sage. He said it might not last that long, but

Monsieur Martin wrapped one up, anyway. We also took a box of treats for Mom and Molly.

I was sad to leave the bakery, but we had to meet Mom and Molly for a little more shopping. I didn't understand what was so great about shopping. How could anything be better than tasting and smelling things in the kitchen of a French bakery?

When we finally got back to Mémé's house, my feet hurt, and I was feeling a bit sick from all the pastries. I sat on my bed and took out the croissant I saved for Sage. It was all crushed, which

made me a little sad. I missed him. I
didn't want to tell anyone that, though.
Especially not Camille, since it was her
birthday the next day.

Camille came in while I was lying
on the bed staring up at the ceiling.
She looked at me. "Phoebe," she said.

"Yeah?" I answered, my lids half
closed.

"Are you okay?" she asked.

"Of course," I said, still staring at
the ceiling.

"Are you sure? You seemed a little sad when we came home. Is it the chocolate croissants? I was really bad at making them when I first tried."

I sat up in bed. "Do you think I was *really* bad at making them?"

"No," she said in a small voice.

"I guess we're not as alike as I thought," I said, my head down. I picked up Josephine and hugged her, but her hard hands poked at me a little bit, so I put her down.

"No, we are! That's just one little thing," she said.

Sage and I were so the same, we never even had to think about it. "I think I just have that disease my mom said people get on jet planes. You know the one that makes you really tired?"

"You mean jet lag?" she said.

"Yeah, that's it," I said.

"I have it, too," she replied.

"Yeah, well, maybe we'll be cured tomorrow."

"Hopefully," she said, and lay down on her bed. After a few minutes she spoke.

"I think I'm feeling better. Do you want to play cards with Mémé?"

"Okay," I said, and tried to rub the jet lag out of my eyes. I did like playing cards. "I'll be down in one minute, okay?"

"Okay," she said cheerfully, and went down the stairs.

I took out the little stack of postcards Dad gave me to send people, got my pen, and started writing.

Dear Sage,
I hope you won't be too jealous to hear this, but I tried five different kinds of pastries at Mr. Durand's old bakery today, and we saw a huge museum called

the Looove with really big statues in it. I saved you a chocolate croissant, but it got smushed in my pocket. How's your ski trip? I'm feeling jealous just thinking about it. By the way, do you think we're a lot alike? Just wondering.
Love, Phoebe

Writing the postcard made me feel a little better. I folded it and put it in my pocket. Then I went downstairs.

Chapter Five

The next morning, I woke up thinking I was in my house. Then I looked over at Camille hugging Juliette tight, and I remembered we were still far away in France. I felt a little pang in my stomach, but it wasn't because I was hungry. I think I missed home.

I got out of bed and sat on the edge of Camille's bed. "Are you awake?" I asked. She didn't answer.

"Camille," I said louder, "are you awake?" and tapped her with Josephine's hand.

"Uh-huh," she mumbled and turned over.

"Happy birthday!" I said, plopping myself on her bed. I wanted to make today special for Camille.

"Thanks, Phoebe," she said, sitting up and brushing the hair out of her eyes. "Guess what we're going to do today?

We're going to Musée de la Poupée and then we get to go out to my favorite restaurant for dinner. Chez Joséphine, just like the doll!"

I blinked at her. "What's a 'musay de la poo-pay'?" I asked.

"It's a museum full of dolls! We used to live near there, and my mom took me all the time," Camille said, and hugged Juliette tight. My heart sank a little. Another museum. Full of dolls. And no Eiffel Tower.

"Aren't you excited?" she asked me, her eyes looking very big and overstimulated.

"I am," I said, trying to sound excited.

"Can you guys quiet down?" Molly
moaned. "Ow, Phoebe, you're standing on
my hair!"

"Oh, sorry," I said to Molly. I kind of
forgot she was right under me on the
floor.

Camille and I went downstairs, and Mémé had another wonderful breakfast waiting for us: big bowls of hot chocolate, dishes of creamy yogurt, blueberries, and more baguettes with butter and apricot jam. Afterward, I asked Camille which of my favorite card games she wanted to play, since it was her birthday.

"Go Fish?" she asked. I nodded, even though my most favorite card game is Crazy Eights. But I did a big compromise because Mom and Dad always say that's what makes a good marriage, and being best friends is kind of like being married. We played that for a while and then Camille opened her presents.

This is what she got:

1 A new sparkly headband, four sparkly barrettes, and a pack of sparkly lip gloss. It's not what I would have wanted, but Camille went wild over them.

2 Two storybooks that had all the words in French from Mémé, which were nice, but a little too French for me.

3 Mom, Dad, and Molly gave her a new red hat, scarf, and gloves, which go perfectly with her cheeks.

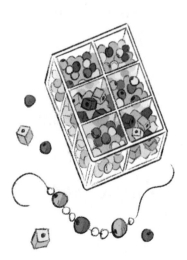

4 And her best present, a jewelry-making kit with real glass beads from—you guessed it— me!

Camille looked very happy, which made me happy, too, even though it wasn't my birthday.

"Now, Phoebe," Mom said later, "in French restaurants, children have to act extra grown-up and sit quietly. Do you think you can do that?"

"Sure thing, Mom, especially if I wear my beret. Then I'll be extra French!"

Later that day, we went to the Musay de la Poopay and saw lots of dolls, some of which were really old and cool looking, but some were kind of boring. After a while I sat down on a bench. I had seen all the dolls I wanted to see.

I took out my postcard to Sage and read
it again.

"Phoebe, isn't this amazing?"
Camille came over and sat next to me,
her cheeks as red as cherries.

"Yeah," I said, and smiled a tired
smile, stuffing the postcard back into
my pocket.

"You don't think so, do you?" Camille
said, her smile fading.

"No, I do!" I said. "I'm just tired.
You know, jet-lag disease."

She nodded. "Yeah."

So we sat there for a minute feeling
sad about our jet-lag disease, but then
Camille was up again, not jet laggy at all.

"Let me show you my favorite doll!" She pulled my arm. I got up.

"Okay," I said and went with her. *It's her birthday, it's her birthday, it's her birthday,* I kept saying in my mind.

It was dark outside when we left the museum.

"We can walk from here," Mrs. Durand said.

We walked and walked. Mr. and Mrs. Durand pointed out lots more fancy French buildings to Mom and Dad. We walked on a little bridge over the Seine, which is a whole river that goes right through Paris. Everyone

oohed and aahed. My parents had
their arms around each other. Mr. and
Mrs. Durand held hands. Molly kept
throwing a new scarf she'd bought
around her neck like she was
a movie star, but I didn't get what was
so great about walking forever in the
cold. I didn't even see the Eiffel Tower
anywhere.

When I was bored or cold, skipping usually helped, so I started to skip, and Camille started skipping with me, and then the walk got much better.

When we arrived at the restaurant, I put on my most grown-up smile and walked up to the lady at the little desk in the front of the restaurant. *"Bonjour, je m'appelle* Phoebe," I said, and gave her a kiss on each cheek just the way the Durands and Mémé did every time they

 said hello to someone. Everyone looked surprised. They had probably never seen me act so grown-up.

Then we followed the lady to our table. She pulled out chairs for everyone, so I started pulling them out, too, just to be extra polite.

"It's okay, Phoebe, our hostess will seat us," said Mrs. Durand with a smile that looked like it was hurting her face.

My mom leaned in close and whispered in my ear. "Phoebe, remember what I said."

"I *am* remembering," I whispered back.

I sat in between Molly and Camille and crossed my legs, put my napkin on my lap, and straightened my beret. I tried to sit very still. Whenever Camille

or Molly moved or talked,
I said, "Shhhh," to them
and looked straight ahead.
"Phoebe," Molly said.
"It's okay for us to talk."

It was good that Molly said that,
because I was about to burst. Everyone
was talking around me. I looked at
the menu. It was all in French, and I
couldn't read a thing.

"Mom? Excuse me?" I said quietly
and very grown-up-like, but she and
Mrs. Durand were talking.

"Dad," I asked again quietly, but he
was talking to Mr. Durand and didn't
hear me.

"Camille? Molly?" I asked, but Camille was saying something to Molly and they didn't hear me.

I decided to tap my water glass with my fork. I had seen a grown-up do that at a wedding once when she wanted to get everyone's attention.

It didn't really make a sound, so I tapped a few more times. It made a bigger sound but still not loud enough, so I tapped even harder. This time it made a sound so loud, not only did my table get quiet, but the whole entire restaurant got quiet and looked at our table. Camille put her hand over her mouth. Mom looked like she might faint.

"Phoebe!" Dad said.

"Um, sorry," I said very quietly, trying to be as grown-up as I could. Then I whispered, "I just wanted to say I can't read the menu." I recrossed my legs and straightened my beret.

"Well, someone's excited to eat," Mr. Durand said, laughing his big laugh. "Let's get started. Why don't I order for us?"

Mom nodded fast and smiled. Dad wiped his forehead with his napkin, and Molly bit her lip.

After I had tried hard to eat bread without getting any crumbs anywhere, the plates started to come. It was like being at a circus full of food. There was pâté, which is kind of like tasting wonderful cat food, more chewy delicious bread, bouillabaisse, crispy duck legs, creamy potatoes, and a whole entire fish on a platter. No matter how different or weird something looked, it always tasted super good. Then a waiter came and placed a plate of something really funny-looking in front of Camille.

"It's my favorite!" Camille exclaimed, clapping her hands.

"What is it?" I asked, leaning over. It looked like a bunch of little shells in some kind of sauce.

"Escargots," she said. "Want a taste?"

"Oh phew, I thought they looked like snails!" I said.

"They are snails," Molly said.

I froze. "Really?"

"They're so good," Camille said. "Just try one." Camille used her little fork that came with the plate of snails to take a snail out of its shell and held it up. It was covered in a greenish sauce that smelled pretty good.

"I, I don't know," I said, and

scrunched up my face without even
meaning to.

"Why are you
making a weird face,
Phoebe?" she asked.

"Well, isn't eating
snails kind of . . .
gross?" I said.

"I never thought so," she
said, looking sad all of a sudden and
putting the snail back down on her
plate.

"Okay, okay, I'll taste it," I said, not
wanting Camille to be sad, especially
on her birthday.

"Good," she said, holding up the

piece again. "Phoebe, you have to open your mouth."

I nodded, but I just couldn't. Snails were slimy. Molly and I found them stuck to rocks around the pond near our house.

"Maybe I'll taste them next year on your birthday?" I offered.

Camille put down her fork again. "But I thought you liked to try new foods just the way I do," she said, looking upset. I thought so, too. She ate a little bit of her snails, and we didn't really talk after that. Even when the chocolate mousse tart came, and everyone sang her a fancy French birthday song, she didn't look that happy and neither did I.

Maybe Camille and I really weren't that alike after all. Her room was pink; mine was purple. She was pretty quiet; I was loud. She loved dolls; I thought

they were just okay. She could make chocolate croissants as good as a pastry chef, and her favorite food was snails. They certainly weren't my favorite food. Did that mean we couldn't be best friends?

Chapter Six

When we got home, Camille
went straight upstairs.

"Phoebe," my mom said.
"Can I talk to you?"

I nodded and followed her
into the kitchen. We sat on
the blue wooden chairs.

"Is anything wrong? You
and Camille seemed a little
down at the end of the night."

"No," I said, not looking at her, my eyes starting to feel a little watery.

"You sure?" she asked.

"I'm just very sick with jet disease," I said, a few tears sneaking out.

"You mean jet lag?" she asked, handing me a tissue. "It's not a disease, sweetie. It just means your body is trying to catch up with France time."

"Oh," I said, blowing my nose. "I think I ruined Camille's birthday."

"Why?"

"Because I was bored at the doll museum and I didn't want to eat her snails," I said. "Does that mean I'm not a foodie? Because if I'm not a foodie, Camille and I might not be best friends."

"Phoebe," Mom said. "Look at me."

I looked. Mom's eyes were soft and nice. She put her hand on my shoulder.

"You don't have to be a foodie if you don't want to. But I saw you try everything other than the snails. Even foodies don't like certain things."

"Really?" I said.

"Of course. Also, you and Camille don't have to like all the same things to be friends."

"But we're *best* friends," I said.

"Doesn't that mean we're alike?"

"You and Sage have been best friends for a long time, and you're pretty different."

I thought about that. I remembered that Sage only liked about five foods, and I liked a million. I also didn't really care about soccer that much, and he was super into it. I was better at math and writing, and Sage was better

at science and art. Sage and I *were* really different.

"Go talk to Camille," Mom said, interrupting

my thoughts. "She looked pretty sad going upstairs. It *is* her birthday."

I wiped my tears and nodded. This was turning out to be one of the longest birthdays of another person ever.

I went upstairs. The door to our little bedroom was closed. I knocked. Camille opened the door. Her eyes and cheeks looked red, but not from being happy.

"Hi, Camille. I'm sorry I didn't eat the snails. I promise I'll try again."

Camille sat down on her bed and hugged Juliette. I came in and sat down on mine.

"I guess I was just afraid that if you
didn't like the doll museum or my
favorite food, I was wondering if you
liked me anymore," she said.

"That's funny. I was afraid that you
wouldn't like me anymore if I didn't
like those things," I told her.

"Oh," she said, wiping her nose.

I tried to remember what my mom told me. "Camille," I said in my most caring voice, "best friends don't have to like each other." Camille's face got all scrunched up again. "Wait, no, that's not what I meant!" I bonked my head with my hand. "I *meant* that best friends don't have to like all the same things. Sage and I like lots of different things, and we've been best friends forever." Her face turned back to a normal color.

"I like how you say the things out loud that I'm afraid to say," Camille explained.

"I like that you make playing with dolls really fun," I said.

"And you're still a foodie even if you don't want to eat snails," she told me.

"I hope so! So are we still best friends?" I asked.

"Forever," she said.

Then we played with Josephine and Juliette and made up a story where they go to France and like different things but have a great time, anyway.

Toward the end of the trip, I wasn't even jet-lag sick anymore. I still missed home and Sage, but most of the time we were having so much fun, I didn't think about it. This is what we did on our last day:

1 We had another delicious lunch of foods with people names, like Quiche Lorraine and Madeleine cookies for dessert, so I got to check everything off my food list. Camille and I rode a Ferris wheel in a beautiful park,

and it turns out we both love
Ferris wheels!

2 A person on the Ferris wheel
was wearing a beret. So I
screamed to Molly, who was
in another seat, because
I wanted to show her, but
then they had to stop the

Ferris wheel because they thought something was wrong with me.

③ We finally went to the top of the Eiffel Tower and looked over all of Paris. It was the most beautiful thing ever and very overstimulating.

"I don't want to leave," Camille said to me as we looked out at the whole entire city.

"I don't, either," I said. "But I'm really glad we're leaving together."

"Me too," she said, smiling. Then Mémé came over to us and patted our backs.

"Look at you sweet girls," she said. "You're like, how do the Americans say? Like two peas in a pod."

"I think maybe you mean we're like a pea and a carrot," I said to Mémé.

"I do?" she asked.

"Yes, totally different vegetables that go perfectly together!" I said.

Mémé still looked a little confused, but Camille grinned.

"You said what I was thinking!" she exclaimed. Then her cheeks turned red and she gave me a big hug.

Veera Hiranandani is the author of *The Night Diary* (Kokila), which has received many accolades including the 2019 Newbery Honor Award. She is also the author of *The Whole Story of Half a Girl* (Yearling), which was named a Sydney Taylor Notable Book and a South Asia Book Award Highly Commended selection. She earned her MFA in fiction writing at Sarah Lawrence College. A former book editor at Simon & Schuster, she now teaches creative writing and is the proud mom of two foodies, who even like to eat their vegetables (most of the time).

Christine Almeda is a Filipino American freelance illustrator and character designer from New Jersey, mainly known for her work in children's books. She believes in the power of creativity and diverse storytelling, and that art can make life more beautiful.